PEPITO'S STORY

to my own
PEPITO
and
ESTRELLITA

COPYRIGHT © 1960 by EUGENE A. FERN
LIBRARY OF CONGRESS CATALOG CARD NUMBER 60-5251
ISBN 0-374-35808-7
PUBLISHED SIMULTANEOUSLY IN CANADA
MANUFACTURED IN THE U.S.A.

Pepito's Story

written and illustrated by

EUGENE FERN

FARRAR, STRAUS AND GIROUX

ARIEL BOOKS • NEW YORK

Padingo was a little fishing town, right by the sea. It was a wonderful place to live, especially for children, because there were so many things to do. There was the sea to swim and fish in, the long, sandy beaches to dig in, mountains to climb, trees to swing from, and even woods to hide in.

So most of the children of Padingo spent their time swimming, fishing, and playing games. All except one little boy, named Pepito. He was different. There was only one thing he really liked to do, and that was — to dance!

When he was dancing, Pepito felt as if he could be anything at all. He could be a king, or a clown; a lion, or a mouse; or a pirate with gold rings in his ears. He could be a seagull in flight or a blade of grass, or the wind itself, when it blows on the sea. There was nothing he couldn't be, when he was dancing. Was it any wonder he loved to dance?

But in spite of his dancing, Pepito was not happy. The reason was simple. No one would dance with him, and so he was quite lonely. He made a rather funny sight dancing all by himself, and the children often laughed at him. This made him feel even worse, though he tried hard not to show it, and sometimes it was easier just to run away and hide in the woods…

. . . or
on
a
lonely
part
of
the
beach.

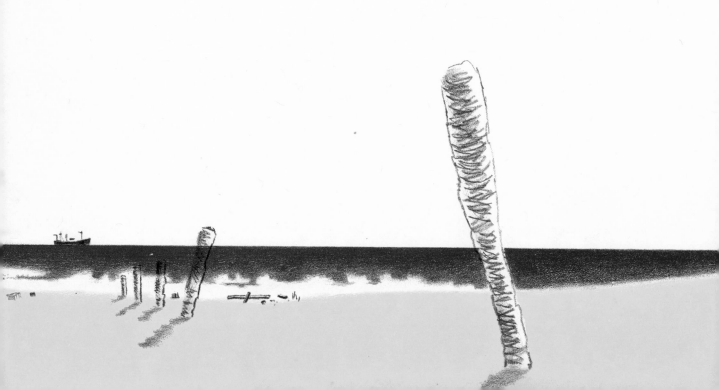

There was one person who
understood Pepito, and that was
his grandmother. She was very old
and as wise as she was old. When
Pepito felt particularly unhappy
about being so different from the
others, and being laughed at, she
would take him in her arms and
repeat this little rhyme:

If every child were like every other,
You wouldn't know who was your sister or brother.
And if every flower looked just the same,
"Flower" would have to be each flower's name.

Pepito didn't know exactly what this meant, but
somehow it always made him feel better.

High on a hill in Padingo there lived a very rich man
named Don Esquadrille and his only daughter,
Estrellita. Besides being a very rich man,
Don Esquadrille had just been made Lord Mayor
of Padingo, and he was very pleased with
himself. He thought nothing too good
for himself or for Estrellita, whom
he loved with all his heart.

Now, Don Esquadrille was a proud man, and much as he loved his daughter, he decided that it would not do for her to play with the children who lived by the sea and spent their time swimming, fishing, and climbing on the rocks. She was the Lord Mayor's daughter, and much too grand for such companions. And since there was no one good enough to play with her, she played with no one at all.

Poor little Estrellita! She had all the dolls and toys a girl could desire, and not a soul to share them with. Sometimes she would stand and look out her window at the sea, remembering the good times she had had playing with the other children, before her father had become Lord Mayor of Padingo.

Day after day went by, until she became quite ill, and had to be put to bed. Don Esquadrille called in all sorts of doctors, but none of them could tell what the matter was, so all their remedies failed. The poor child grew thinner and weaker by the day. At last her father asked if there was anything at all he could do to make her feel better. Estrellita replied, "Yes, Father. I would like to see my friends — the children who live by the sea."

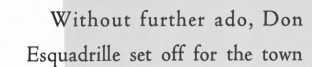

Without further ado, Don Esquadrille set off for the town square. He gathered all the children together and told them of Estrellita's wish. He asked them to come to his house, and urged each child to bring some gift to cheer her up. "Perhaps if she had a real friend," he said to himself, "she would try to get well."

The children scurried off in all directions in search of presents. They loved Estrellita, and each child hoped that his gift would be the one to make her raise her head and smile. Only Pepito stood there uncertainly, wondering what to do.

Pepito and his grandmother were very poor, and the boy could think of nothing he could give Estrellita. As he trudged sadly home, Pepito remembered that he had a special reason for loving Estrellita. Of all the children in Padingo, she alone had never made fun of his dancing.

If only he could think of some way to help her! He thought and thought, and when he could think no more, he started to cry.

When his grandmother heard what was the matter, she said, "No doll or toy will make Estrellita well. What she needs is something very special — something you alone can give." And taking him in her arms, she repeated the little rhyme:

If every child were like every other,
You wouldn't know who was your sister or brother;
And if every flower looked just the same,
"Flower" would have to be each flower's name.

This time Pepito nodded, for all at once he had an idea.

Drying his eyes and standing up tall, Pepito marched up the hill that led to the home of Don Esquadrille. He knocked firmly at the big front door, and soon he was standing in a hall filled with children, all holding in their arms the gifts they had brought for Estrellita.

One by one the children tiptoed into Estrellita's bedroom and presented their gifts. Estrellita thanked them all very nicely, and they tiptoed quietly out. Don Esquadrille watched her face hopefully . . .

. . . but it was as sad and pale as ever.

Just then, in walked Pepito, alone as usual.
His hands were empty, but he was smiling. He
looked at Estrellita, quite lost in the big bed, her
little face almost the color of the pillow. His dark
eyes glowed with feeling, but he said nothing.
Instead, he started to dance.

Pepito danced as he had never danced before! Into his dancing he poured
everything in his heart: the loneliness of the little girl living on the hill, his

own loneliness among the other children, his sorrow that she was sick, and
his hope that she would soon be well and able to play with her friends again.

…As he danced, a strange thing happened. Estrellita began to smile, at first only with her eyes, but soon it was with her whole face. All of a sudden she laughed, clapped her hands, and sat up in bed.

A moment later she had thrown back the cover and jumped to the floor. No sooner was she on her feet than she began to dance with Pepito! Don Esquadrille rubbed his

eyes, but when he saw that it was really true, that his beloved daughter was well again, he was so overjoyed that he joined hands with the two children and began to dance himself!

Never had the house on the hill been filled with such joy! The Lord Mayor was happy once more because Estrellita was well, and also because he had learned something: that no amount of presents can take the place of real friendship.

From that night on, Estrellita could play
with anyone she liked, and she was never
lonely or sick again. She spent long days by
the sea with her many friends—but most of
all with her special friend, Pepito.

As for Pepito, well...

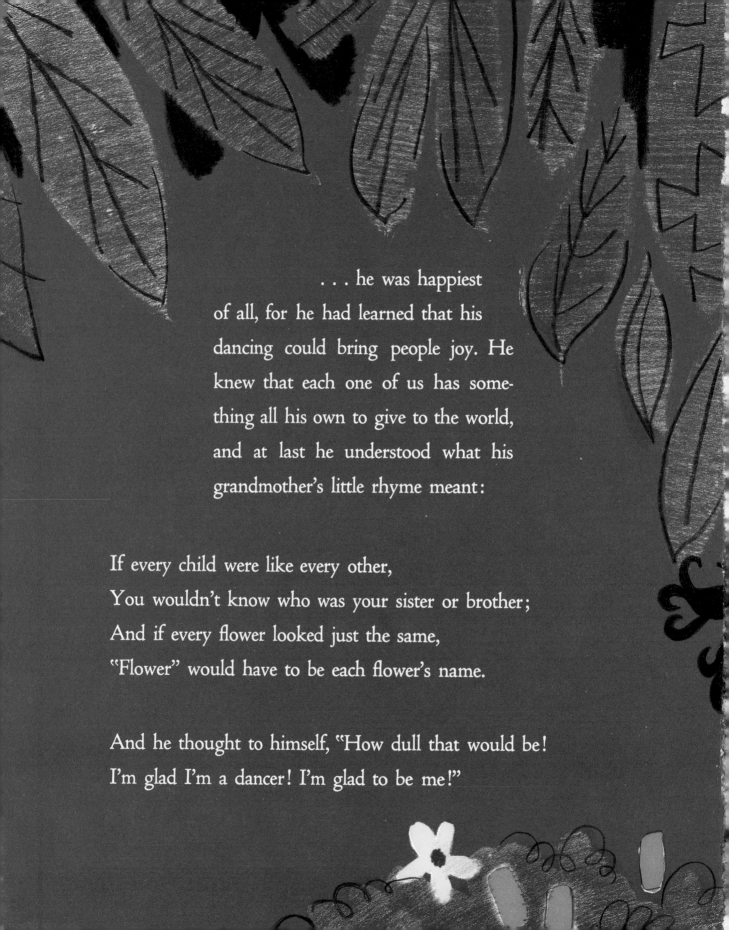

. . . he was happiest
of all, for he had learned that his
dancing could bring people joy. He
knew that each one of us has something all his own to give to the world,
and at last he understood what his
grandmother's little rhyme meant:

If every child were like every other,
You wouldn't know who was your sister or brother;
And if every flower looked just the same,
"Flower" would have to be each flower's name.

And he thought to himself, "How dull that would be!
I'm glad I'm a dancer! I'm glad to be me!"